D1429202

a 3 0 1 1 8 0 1 0 7 5 6 7 5 1 b

THE LITTLE MISERY

The collected English edition
of the novels of FRANÇOIS MAURIAC

A WOMAN OF THE PHARISEES (La Pharisienne)

THÉRÈSE (Thérèse Desqueyroux, *two stories from* Plongées *and* La Fin de la Nuit)

THE UNKNOWN SEA (Les Chemins de la Mer)

THE DESERT OF LOVE (Le Desert de l'Amour) *and* THE ENEMY (Le Mal) *in one volume*

A KISS FOR THE LEPER (Le Baiser au Lépreux) *and* GENETRIX (Genitrix) *in one volume*

THAT WHICH WAS LOST (Be qui était perdu) *and* THE DARK ANGELS (Les Anges Noirs) *in one volume*

THE KNOT OF VIPERS (Le Nœud de Vipères)

THE LITTLE MISERY (Le Sagouin)

In preparation

THE FRONTENAC MYSTERY (Le Mystère Frontenac)

FRANÇOIS MAURIAC

THE LITTLE MISERY

(Le Sagouin)

Translated by
GERARD HOPKINS

LONDON
EYRE & SPOTTISWOODE

First published in French 1951
This first English edition 1952

This book is made and printed in Great Britain for Eyre & Spottiswoode (Publishers) Ltd., 15 Bedford Street, London, W.C.2, by Staples Printers Ltd., Rochester, Kent.

THE LITTLE MISERY

CHAPTER I

I

"WHY go on saying that you know your lesson, when it's quite obvious that you don't? . . . You just learned it off by heart, didn't you now?"

There was the sound of a slap.

"Go to your room, and don't let me set eyes on you till dinner-time!"

The child raised his hand to his face and felt it gingerly, as though his jaw had been broken.

"Ooh! that did hurt!" (he might as well make the most of his advantage) "I'll tell Mamie, you see if I don't! . . ."

In an access of fury, Paula grabbed her son's skinny arm, and administered a second slap.

"Mamie, eh? . . . well, here's something for you to go whining to your *father* about! . . . what are you waiting for? . . . get out of my sight!"

She pushed him into the passage, shut the door, then opened it again to fling lesson-books and notebooks after the retreating Guillaume. Still snivelling, he squatted down on his heels and picked them up. There was a sudden silence: not so much as the sound of a snuffle in the darkness. At last she had got rid of him!

She listened to his departing footsteps. It was pretty certain that he would not seek refuge with his father, and, since his grandmother, his "Mamie", was out, pleading his cause with the schoolmaster, it would be the kitchen he'd make for, to get a little sympathy from Fraülein. He was probably at it already, taking a surreptitious lick at the cooking food under the sentimental eyes of the Austrian woman. 'I can as good as see him doing it. . . .' What Paula saw, when she thought about her son, was a picture of knock-knees, skinny legs, and socks festooned untidily over his boots. This little scrap of humanity, this flesh of her flesh, had eyes the colour of ripe blackberries, but of them she took no account. On the other hand, she was horribly conscious, with bitter loathing, of the sagging, adenoidal mouth and the drooling lower lip. It was less prominent than his father's, but it was enough for Paula that it reminded her of a mouth she hated.

Rage flooded her mind – rage? – or was it just exasperation? It is no easy thing to tell where exasperation ends and hate begins. She went back into the room, and paused for a moment in front of the wardrobe looking-glass. Each year, when Autumn came round, she put on the same old knitted jersey of greenish wool which had grown too big for her round the neck. No amount of cleaning could keep the stains from re-appearing. The brown skirt, spattered with mud, stuck out in front as though she were with child – though, thank God, there was no fear of that!

"Baronne de Cernès" – she muttered to herself – "the Baronne Galéas de Cernès. Paula de Cernès." Her lips parted in a smile which brought no gaiety to the bilious cheeks with their thick growth of down (the Cernès urchins made a great joke of Madame Galéas's whiskers!). She stood there, laughing to herself, and thinking of the girl she once had been who, thirteen years earlier, before another mirror, had stood nerving herself to take the plunge with repetition of the selfsame words: "The Baron and the Baronne Galéas de Cernès . . . *M. Constant Meulière, sometime Mayor of Bordeaux, and Madame Meulière, take pleasure in announcing the marriage of their niece, Paula Meulière, to the Baron Galeas de Cernès.*"

Neither uncle nor aunt, eager though they were to be rid of her, had urged the taking of that lunatic step. They had even warned her against it. What school influence was it that had bred in her a weakness for titles? – to what pressure had she yielded? To-day she could find no answer to that question. Perhaps mere curiosity had been the reason, or the longing to force an entry into a forbidden world. . . . She had never forgotten the groups of aristocratic children in the City Park – the Curzays, the Pichon-Longuevilles – in whose games there could never have been a question of her joining. The Mayor's niece had circled in vain about those arrogant scions of a nobler race . . . "Mamma says we mustn't play with you . . ." The grown girl had, no doubt, sought to avenge the snubbed child. Her marriage, she had thought, would open a way for her into the unknown, would be the harbour from which she could set sail for unimagined splendours. She knew all right, to-day, what people meant when they spoke of "closed circles": only too well she knew! To enter this one had seemed hard enough, almost impossible – but not so hard, not so impossible, as to get out of it again!

And for that she had thrown away her life! To have said she felt at moments a regret, would have been to indulge in understatement! Even obsession was too weak a word! Her hideous fate had only too real a body. Never a moment passed but she was conscious of it. It was there to be seen, the embodiment of idiotic vanity, of criminal stupidity, the sign and symbol of an ineluctable destiny. To make matters worse, she was not even "Madame la Baronne". There was only one Madame la Baronne, her ancient mother-in-law. Paula would never be anything but Madame Galéas. Her imbecile husband's outlandish name had become her own, so that she was bound still closer, if that were possible, to the ruin she had married and made her own for ever.

At night, the mockery of her life, the horror that came

with the thought that she had sold herself for a golden vanity of which she could not enjoy even the shadow, filled her mind and kept her sleepless until morning. If she sought distraction in imagined fantasies – not seldom filthy – the rock-bottom of her thought remained immoveable. All night long she lay in the darkness, struggling to clamber from the pit into which she had fallen of her own free will, knowing there was no escape. Whatever the season of the year, night for her was always the same. In the Carolina poplars near the window the owls in Autumn hooted to the moon like baying dogs, but they were infinitely less hateful than the implacable nightingales of Spring. The sense of rage, of desperation at having been duped was always waiting for her when she woke, especially in Winter, to the sound of Fraülein's heavy-handed drawing of the curtains. Emerging from the mists of sleep, she saw through the windows a few ghosts of trees, still hung with tattered leaves, waving their blackened branches in the eddying fog.

And yet, those were the best times of her day, those morning moments when she could lie torpid in the snug warmth of the half-deserted bed. Little Guillaume was only too glad to forget the duty of the day's first kiss. Quite often Paula could hear, beyond the door, the voice of the old Baronne, urging the boy to go in and say good morning to his mother. Though she detested her daughter-in-law, she would make no compromise with principle. Then, Guillaume would slip into the room, and stand for a moment on the threshold, all eyes for the terrifying head upon the pillows with its hair drawn tightly back upon the temples to reveal a narrow, vaguely defined forehead, and a yellow cheek (with the mole nestling in a tuft of black hair) to which he would hastily press his lips. He knew in advance that his mother would wipe away the hasty salutation, and say, with disgust sounding in her voice – "you always make me so wet…"

She no longer struggled against that feeling of disgust. Was it her fault that she could get nothing from the wretched creature? What could she do with a sly and backward oaf who always knew that his grandmother and old Fraülein would back him up? But now even the Baronne was growing sensible. She had agreed to see what she could do with the schoolmaster – an irreligious schoolmaster, to be sure, but that couldn't be helped. The curé had three parishes to serve, and lived over a mile away. On two separate occasions, once in 1917, and again in 1918, they had tried the experiment of boarding Guillaume away from home, first with the Jesuits at Sarlat, then at a small Seminary in the Lower Pyrenees. But he had been sent back after a term. The nasty little creature soiled his sheets. Neither the Jesuits, nor the Seminarists, were equipped, especially not just then, to deal with backward, or with sickly, boys.

How would this schoolmaster, with his curly hair and laughing eyes, this veteran of Verdun, welcome the old Baronne? Would he feel flattered that she had put herself out for him? Paula had managed to get herself excused. She lacked the courage now to face strangers, least of all this brilliant teacher. She was terrified of him. The Cernès bailiff, Arthur Lousteau, though a strong adherent of the *Action francaise*, was full of admiration for him, was convinced that he would go far. . . . The old Baronne, like all the country gentry, thought Paula, had a way with the "natives". She knew the subtleties of local patois. One of the few things about her which still had power to charm was the outworn elegance with which spoke that ancient tongue. . . . Yes, but this socialist schoolmaster had other origins, and the Baronne's excessive affability might seem to him insulting. The affected pretence of appearing not to notice social differences no longer appealed to young men of his type. Still, after all, he had been wounded at Verdun, and that would create a bond with the old lady, whose younger son, Georges de Cernès has been reported "missing" in Champagne.

Paula opened the window, and saw, at the far end of the avenue, the Baronne's bent, emaciated figure. She was leaning heavily on her stick. A black straw hat was perched high on her piled hair. She moved between the elms which seemed ablaze, herself all glowing in the light of the setting sun. Paula could see that she was talking and gesturing. That she should be so agitated was no good sign. The young woman went down the great double staircase which was the glory of Cernès, and met her in the hall.

"A boor, my dear, as was only to be expected."

"Did he refuse? Are you sure you didn't rub him up the wrong way. I do hope you didn't put on your grand manner . . . I told you . . ."

The elder lady shook her head, but her denial was only the automatic protest of the very old, which seems to be saying "No" to death. An artificial white flower trembled ludicrously on her straw hat. Her eyes were dim with tears which would not flow.

"What excuse did he make?"

"He said that he was too busy . . . that his work as the Mayor's secretary left him no leisure. . . ."

"He must have cooked up a better story than that. . . ."

"I assure you that he did not. He spoke only of his work. He didn't, he said, want anything to 'interfere with it' . . ."

The Baronne de Cernès clung heavily to the banisters, and kept stopping for breath. Her daughter-in-law followed slowly, climbing the stairs behind her, questioning her all the time with that nagging obstinacy of which she was so little aware. She noticed, however, that she was frightening the old lady, and made an effort to lower her voice. But the words still hissed between her clenched teeth.

"Why did you say at first that he behaved like a boor?"

The Baronne sat down on the landing sofa. She was still shaking her head, and a grimace, which might have been a smile, was agitating her lips. Paula raised her voice again: had she, or had she not, accused the schoolmaster of boorishness?

"No, my dear, no . . . I was guilty of exaggeration. Maybe I misunderstood. . . . Quite possibly the young man was innocent of intentional offence. . . . I may have read meanings into his words which were not there."

But Paula would not desist. What meanings? What had he said?"

"It was when he asked me why we had not applied to the curé. I told him that the curé does not live here, that he has three parishes on his hands. Do you know what that wretched school-teacher had the effrontery to say? . . . but, no, it'll only make you angry . . ."

"What did he say? I won't give you a moment's peace until you tell me exactly what he said."

"Well, he told me with a snigger that on one point, it seemed, he saw eye to eye with the curé. Neither of them liked entanglements, and he certainly had no intention of getting himself mixed up with the great house. Oh, *I* knew well enough what he meant, and I would have you know that if he hadn't been wounded at Verdun, I would have made him explain himself more explicity. *I'd* have known how to defend you!"

Paula's rage fell suddenly to silence. She hung her head, and, without another word, hurried downstairs, and took her cloak which was hanging in the hall.

The Baronne waited until the front door had closed behind her. This time there was no doubt about the smile which disclosed her discoloured dentures. Leaning over the stair-rail, she spat out the three words – "*That* got you!", and then, in a cracked but piercing voice, cried out suddenly – "Galéas! Guillou! – darlings!"

She was not kept long waiting for an answer. It came from the remote depths of the service wing, from the kitchen: "Mamie! Maminette!" Father and son came dashing up the stairs, making no noise in their stockinged feet. Her call had meant that, for a time at least, the enemy had gone. They could get together now and sit round the lamp in Mamie's room.

Galéas took his mother's arm. He was wearing an old brown woolly. His shoulders were narrow and sloping, his disproportionately large head was covered with a great mat of hair. There was a childlike charm about his eyes, but the drooling, open mouth and thick tongue were horrible. His trousers hung loose above his feet, and sagged in great folds about his skeleton legs.

Guillaume had taken Mamie's other hand, and was rubbing his cheek against it. Of her words he retained only those that concerned him nearly. The schoolmaster didn't want to be bothered with him: he wouldn't have to stand trembling under those appraising eyes. The shadow of that particular monster was growing less. All else that Mamie had said was incomprehensible. "I got a good one in on your mother!" – A good one? what was that? The three of them entered the beloved room. Guillaume made for his corner between the prie-Dieu and the bed. In the back of the prie-Dieu there was a tiny cupboard filled with broken rosaries. One of them, with mother-of-pearl beads, had been blessed by the Pope: another, of olive stones, had been brought back by Mamie from Jerusalem. There was a metal box made in the shape of St. Peter's at Rome. It had been one of Galéas's christening presents, and bore his name in silver letters. There were prayerbooks crammed with pictures showing the smiling features of the dead. Mamie and papa were whispering together under the lamp. A fire of logs threw vivid gleams into the corners of the room. Mamie took from the drawer in the pedestal table a greasy pack of tiny cards.

"We shan't be disturbed until dinner-time, Galéas: you can play the piano."

She was soon absorbed in her game of Patience. The piano had been brought into this room, filled though it was to bursting with assorted furniture, because Paula could not bear to listen to her husband's strumming. Guillaume knew in advance what the tunes would be. His father would play them in exactly the same order. First, the *Turkish Patrol*. Every evening Guillou waited for the same wrong note in the same place. Sometimes Galéas would talk while he was playing. His toneless voice sounded as though it were still at the breaking stage.

"This schoolmaster's a red, isn't he, mamma?" "As red as red – at least, that's what Lousteau says."

The *Turkish Patrol* resumed its uncertain course. A picture rose before Guillaume's eyes of the red man all smeared with ox blood. Not that he didn't know him well by sight – a limping figure, always bare-headed and leaning on a handsome ebony cane. The red must be hidden by his clothes. Red like a fish. The last of the daylight still showed between the drawn curtains. Mama would go wandering about the country till dinner-time, as she always did when she was in a particularly bad temper. She would come back, hatless, with mud on the bottom of her dress. She would smell of sweat. As soon as dinner was over, she would go to bed. They would be able to have a good hour together in front of Mamie's fire. Fraülein came in, tall and fat and flabby. She always found some excuse to join them when the enemy was out tramping the roads. Would they like their chestnuts boiled or roasted? Had she better do an egg for Guillou? She brought with her into grandmamma's room a mixed smell of onions and washing-up. This asking of her employers' wishes was a pure formality. Guillou would have his egg . . . (he had been so called since the war on account of his being unlucky enough to have the same name as the Kaiser – or "késer" as the Baronne pronounced it).

Already they were talking of "her". "She told me my kitchen was dirty . . . so I said that I was mistress in my own kitchen. . . ." Guillaume could see Mamie and Papa stretching their skinny necks, the better to hear what Fraülein was saying. To him it was of no interest whatever, since for other people he felt neither hate nor love. His grandmother, his father, Fraülein provided that climate of security which he found so necessary, from which his mother fought tooth and nail to drive him, like a ferret attacking a rabbit deep in its warren. At no matter what cost, he had got to come out, and, dazed, bewildered, submit to her furious rages. When that happened he just rolled himself into a ball and waited for the storm to pass. Thanks, however, to the state of warfare that was forever smouldering between the grown-ups, he could, to some extent, live his life in peace. He hid behind Fraûlein. The Austrian woman spread over him a bulky shadow of protection. Mamie's bedroom might be a safer refuge than the kitchen, but he knew better than to trust Mamie, or to rely upon the kindness of her words and gestures. Fraûlein was somebody apart. With a love that was half a passion of the flesh, she brooded over her chick, her duckling. She it was who gave him his bath, and soaped him with her old hands, which were so chapped and dirty.

Meanwhile, Paula had turned into the path which led off to the left from the front steps. She reached, unseen, a narrow lane behind the stable-yard. It was almost always deserted. She strode along it like a man. As a rule she went nowhere, but this evening her progress was marked by a strange air of haste. Walking, she could the more easily chew over the words spoken by the schoolmaster, and told her by her mother-in-law, those veiled references to the gossip about her and the late curé. The knowledge that she, and none but she, had built the prison in which she now lived, was a horror ever with her. It might have been tolerable – or so she thought – but for the shame that had fallen upon her during the first year of her married life. Inevitably she was a branded criminal in the eyes of all who saw her. She had been made to bear the burden of a fault which she had not committed, of a fault that was not so much shameful as ridiculous. For once it was not her husband, nor his mother, who was responsible for the ill-natured gossip. Her real enemies lived in a world where vengeance could not reach them. Only at an occasional religious ceremony had she so much as seen them at a distance – those Vicars-General, those Canons of the Church in whose eyes the daughter-in-law of the Baronne de Cernès was a walking danger to the spiritual health of all anointed priests. The scandal was a matter of common knowledge throughout the diocese. It was bandied from mouth to mouth. Already there had been three successive chaplains at Cernès, and each had been reminded by the diocesan authorities that permission to say Mass in the private chapel had been rescinded; that, though there must be no open scandal, they must be careful to avoid familiar discourse with the family (for all its great name) "because of an event that is only too well known to all of us".

For several years now, because of Paula, the Chapel at Cernès had been left unconsecrated. That, in itself, was a matter of complete indifference to the young woman (the distance of the Parish Church had provided her with a blessed excuse for never setting foot in it). But there was not a person within ten miles who did not know why that interdict had been laid upon the family. It was because of the old lady's daughter-in-law – "her as had been caught with the curé". The more indulgent gossipers would add that, actually, no one knew precisely how far things had gone. Probably they had not done anything really *wrong* . . . all the same . . . well, the priest had been sent away, hadn't he?

The tree-trunks were in shadow, but a streak of red still lay low against the sky. It was long since Paula had noticed such things – trees, the sky, the wide stretches of the countryside, though, at times, like any peasant, she would read the signs in nature of a coming storm, of a change in the temperature. Once she had found pleasure in the visible world, but all that part of her had died on the day when, at this very hour, and on this selfsame road, she had walked beside an overgrown innocent, a young, half-famished priest. He had been pushing his bicycle and talking to her in a low voice. The peasants who had seen them pass had had no doubt that love was the burden of their words. But all that had ever happened had been the meeting, in their persons, of two solitary sufferers whose loneliness had never mingled.

Paula had heard the laughter of a group of girls and boys behind a turning in the road. In a moment they would be in sight. She had pressed into the bank so as not to see them, so as not to be seen. She had led her companion into a track which branched off from the lane. It had been a foolish thing to do, because it had at once given rise to suspicion.

This evening, though a damp mist was rising, she sat down among the dead leaves of a chestnut copse, drew her knees up to her chin, and clasped her hands about her legs. Where was he now, that poor young priest? Where was he hiding his suffering? She did not know, but only that, wherever he might be, he would be suffering if he were still alive. No, there had never been anything between them. It was not the thought of *that* which worried her. Brought up in the horror of the priestly habit, such an intrigue would have been for her impossible. Yet, the poor imbeciles who lived about had classed her – and with authority to back them – among those mad and sex-starved women who make themselves a burden to the clergy. Nothing she could do would ever tear that label from her neck. But what of him? Had he in any way been guilty? He had responded to the confidences of a young, despairing woman, not with the grave words of a spiritual director, but with confidences returned. That had been the sum-total of his wrongdoing. She had sought help from him, as she had had a perfect right to do – and he had welcomed her like some shipwrecked mariner seeing a companion in misfortune land upon his desert isle.

The poor young priest, still little more than a rather backward boy, had been the prey of some secret despair, though what its nature was she had never really known.

So far as she could judge (she took very little interest in such matters) he had believed himself to be a useless soul rejected of God. A species of hatred had taken possession of him, hatred of the loutish, unresponsive countryfolk, to whom he could not talk, whose thoughts were bounded by the land they lived by, who had no need of him. Solitude had sent him nearly mad. Yes, quite literally, he was well on the way to going mad through loneliness. No help had come to him from God. He had told Paula that, as a result of emotional transports and a fleeting visitation of Grace, he had believed himself to have a vocation. Once caught in the trap, however, he had never experienced those feelings again. . . . It was as though somebody had laid a bated snare, and then had lost all interest once he was tangled in the net. That, at least, was what Paula had thought he had said. But for her all such concerns belonged to an absurd, an "unthinkable" world. She had listened to his outburst of self-pity with but half an ear, only waiting until he paused for breath to take up the story of her own unhappiness. "And I . . ." she had said, and straight embarked upon the narrative of her marriage. There had been nothing between them but this alternation of monologues. Once only, in the Presbytery garden, and then because he was at the end of his tether, he had, for the space of a few seconds, rested his head upon her shoulder. Almost at once she had slipped away, but not before a neighbour's eye had seen them. That had been the start of the whole business. Because of that single gesture (and it might have changed his whole life) the little lamp was never more to burn before the altar in the family Chapel. The old Baronne had scarcely even protested against the interdict. It was as though she found it natural that the presence of God at Cernès should be thought incompatible with that of the daughter-in-law who had been born a Meulière.

Paula was beginning to feel cold. It was growing dark under the chestnuts. She got up, shook out her skirt, and went back to the path. One of the towers of the great house, dating from the fourteenth century, could be seen from here between the pines. But by now the night was so dark that even this descendant of a race of muleteers could no longer make it out.

For twelve years she had borne upon her back the burden of this calumny, knowing it to be in everybody's mouth. But suddenly the thought that it had reached the ears of a schoolmaster to whom she had never so much as spoken, seemed to her to be beyond all bearing. She knew every man by sight for miles around. There was scarcely one of them she would have failed to recognize at a distance. But the picture of that curly head must have forced its way, almost without her knowledge, into her consciousness – the picture of a schoolmaster whose name was still unknown to her. For schoolmasters and priests have neither of them any need of names. Their function is enough to give them an identity. She could not endure the thought that he should go on believing in this story about her even for one day longer. She would tell him what had really happened. The same imperious need to confess, to lighten herself of a load she could no longer carry, which, twelve years earlier, had led her to confide imprudently in a priest who had been too young and too weak, was nagging at her again. She must fight down her shyness. She must take up the cudgels once again for Guillaume. Perhaps the schoolmaster would yield. In any case, she would have made contact with him. A bond might form between them.

She hung up her cloak in the hall. By force of habit she washed her hands at the scullery sink, then went into the servant's sitting-room, where the family, since the death of Georges, the younger son, had taken to having their meals. The official dining-room, a vast and icy cold apartment, was never used except during the Christmas holidays, and in September, when the Baronne's eldest daughter, the Comtesse d'Arbis, came from Paris with her children and Georges' little daughter, Danièle. On the occasion of those visits, the two garden-boys were put into livery: a cook was engaged: a pair of saddle horses was hired.

This evening, Paula did not go straight to the smaller dining-room. Eager to reopen as soon as possible the argument about the schoolmaster, she made her way instead to her mother-in-law's room. She entered it, perhaps, ten times in the year. She stood now behind the closed door listening to the gay babble of the three conspirators within, to the sound of a tune which Galéas was playing with one finger. Something that Fraûlein had just said produced a burst of laughter from the old Baronne. How Paula hated that forced, affected titter! She opened the door without knocking. Like the wooden figures on a public clock those in the room were smitten into sudden immobility. The Baronne sat for a moment with one hand raised, holding a card. Galéas slammed the cover of the piano and swung round on his stool. Fraûlein turned towards the enemy, looking for all the world like a cat confronted by a dog, its face flattened in a snarl, its ears laid back, its body arched, and just about to spit. Guillou, surrounded by newspapers from which he had been cutting photographs of aeroplanes, put his scissors on the table, and curled up once again between the prie-Dieu and the bed, drawing in his legs, and playing 'possum'.

Never before had Paula realized so clearly – accustomed though she was to such scenes – how baleful an influence she exercised on those with whom she had to live. Almost at once, her mother-in-law recovered from the shock of the surprise, and gave her a twisted smile, exhibiting the same slightly excessive amiability that she would have shown to a stranger of inferior social status. She started fussing about the younger woman's damp feet, and told her to come to the fire. Fraûlein grumblingly muttered something about its not being worth while because she was just going to serve dinner. She made for the door with Galéas and Guillaume hard at her heels. "As usual", thought the Baronne, "they're unloading her on me."

"Have I your permission, my dear, to put on the fireguard?"

She effaced herself in Paula's presence, and, not for the world would ever have left a room in front of her daughter-in-law. All the way into dinner she talked incessantly, making it impossible, until they were all at table, for Paula to get a word in edgeways. Galéas and Guillaume were standing by their chairs. As soon as they were seated, they started noisily lapping their soup. The Baronne asked whether they didn't all think it was very mild to-day, adding that it was scarcely ever cold at Cernès in November. She had started making her melon jam that very afternoon. This time she was going to try the experiment of mixing it with apricots.

"The sort my poor, dear Adhémar always called, so

amusingly, old women's ears – do you remember, Galéas?"

She was talking for the sake of talking. All that mattered was that Paula should not be allowed to start arguing again. But watching her, she saw signs of impending trouble on the hateful face. Guillaume sat with hunched shoulders, uneasy under his mother's watchful eyes. He, too, felt that there was danger in the air, and that it had something to do with him. Try though he might to make himself one with the table and the chair, he knew only too well that Mamie's talk would not fill the silence, and could offer only a feeble barrier to the storm already piling up behind the tight lips of the adversary.

Galéas ate and drank without looking up, bending so low over his food that the greying thicket of hair on the enormous head was at Paula's eye-level. He was hungry, having worked all day in the churchyard, which it was his self-imposed task to keep tidy. Thanks to him there were no neglected graves at Cernès. At the moment he was untroubled, since it was not at him that his wife was looking. He was in luck's way. She had banished him from her mind, which meant that he was the only one of the company who could bask at ease and indulge such whims as pouring wine into his soup, and, as he put it, "trying a little of everything." He mashed and munched, piling his plate with everything on the table, and the

Baronne was hard put to it to keep Guillaume from imitating his father without undermining the respect due to him. Papa could do as he liked, she said: but Guillou must sit at table like a well-brought-up little boy. It didn't, in fact, ever occur to him to criticize his father, finding it impossible to imagine him as different from what he was. Papa belonged to a species of grown-ups which threatened no danger. That would have been Guillaume's verdict had he been capable of forming one. Papa never made a noise, never interrupted the stories which Guillaume was for ever telling to himself. Indeed, he became part of them, and was no more intrusive than the dogs and oxen on the farm. His mother, on the other hand, broke in upon them with violence, and stuck there like some foreign body. He was not always conscious of her presence, but he knew that she was there. . . . Suddenly, he heard her speak his name. That had torn it! – they were going to talk about him! She mentioned the schoolmaster. He tried to understand what she was saying. He had been dragged by the ears from his earth, and now lay exposed to the glare of the grown-up world.

"But what do you suggest that we should do with Guillaume, then? Have you any alternative to suggest? Oh, I know he can read and write and just about manage to count . . . but that's not saying much for a twelve-year-old. . . ."

According to the Baronne there was no hurry. They must take their time about thinking what would be best to do.

"But he's already been sent away from two schools. You say that this schoolmaster won't do anything about him. In that case, we must have a tutor for him, at home – or a governesss."

The old lady protested loudly at such an idea. She would not dream of having a stranger in the house . . . she trembled at the mere thought of exposing their life at Cernès to alien eyes – their life as it had become since the day when Galéas had given his name to this Fury! "Perhaps *you* can think of something else, my dear?"

Paula emptied her glass at a gulp and refilled it. Both the Baronne and Fraülein had noticed that, since the first year of her marriage, Paula had shown a fondness for drink. Fraülein had tried making a pencil mark on the bottles of liqueur, so as to check her consumption, but Paula, noticing this, had accumulated in her wardrobe a secret supply of anisette and cherrybrandy, of curaçao and apricot cordial. But this the Austrian woman had discovered. One day, the Baronne had felt it to be her duty to put the dear girl on her guard against strong liquors, but her words had led to such an outburst, that she had never again dared to refer to the subject.

"In my opinion we have no choice but to try again with the schoolmaster . . ."

At that, the Baronne raised her hands, declaring that not for any consideration in the world would she expose herself again to the insolence of that Communist. Paula reassured her. There was no question of that, she said. She, herself, would make the approach, and do her best to suceed where her mother-in-law had failed. She refused to discuss the matter, but said, over and over again, that her mind was quite made up, and that, after all, Guillaume's education was her concern.

"It seems to me that my son might have something to say in the matter!"

"You know that his 'say' will be precisely nothing!"

"If that is how you feel, I have at least the right to insist that you speak to this creature in your own name only. You can, if you like, tell him that I know nothing of your intentions. Should you, however, object to soiling your lips with so white a lie, then I must ask you to make it clear that you are acting contrary to my judgment, and in direct opposition to my wishes."

Paula mockingly suggested that it was the old lady's Christian duty to suffer humiliation for her grandson's sake.

"My dear girl, whatever you have done, or still may do, I wish it to be fully understood that I am in no way involved. I don't wish to be offensive, but no one could well be less a member of the family than you."

Her tone was perfectly polite, and her long upper lip curled in a smile which revealed her fine and rather too regular teeth.

Paula's nerves were frayed, and she found it difficult to contain herself.

"I you wish to imply that I have never shown the slightest wish to resemble the Cernès – you are perfectly right."

"In that case, my dear, there is nothing for you to worry about. No one, I feel sure, has ever done you the wrong of taking you for what you are not."

Guillaume would have liked to slip from the room, but did not dare. Besides, he found this rumbling battle of the gods above his head rather thrilling, though the point of their acid exchanges escaped him.

Galéas got up, leaving the sweet untouched, as he always did when there was cream. The adversaries faced one another.

"It would be a bad day for me if I was to be considered as one of the family when you find the house burning over your head. . . ."

"Are you, by any chance, trying to frighten me? For more than four hundred years the Cernès have always treated their people well, and set a good example. They have been, and are, thank God, loved and respected. . . ."

Indignation had set the old voice trembling.

"Loved? . . . Respected? . . . why, you're hated by the whole village. Your obstinacy in keeping Fraûlein here during the war. . . ."

"Forgive me for smiling. . . . An Austrian of sixty-four, who has lived with us ever since she was a girl! . . . The military authorities thought it wise to shut their eyes – and they were right."

"But the people here are only too glad to have a good excuse. . . . It is quite incredible that anyone should be so wilfully blind! . . . You have always been detested . . . . Do you really think that the tenant-farmers and the tradespeople are taken in by the soft-soap you give them? Because of you, they hate everything you love . . . priests and all. Just you wait and see! . . . Unfortunately, I shall be lumped in with the rest of you. Still, I think I shall die happy!"

She finished by muttering a vulgar phrase which the Baronne had never heard before. "How revealing language can be", thought the old lady, her anger suddenly abated. It sometimes happened that her daughter from Paris, and particularly her grandchildren, would risk using a slang expression in her hearing, but never would they have said anything so common! What, precisely, had it been? – "You're going to get it in the neck!" –

yes, that was it. As always, Paula's displays of temper had a calming effect on the old lady. She recovered the advantage which self-control enjoys when at odds with hysteria.

"I would not have you think for a moment that your hatred of the aristocracy surprises me. No matter what may be your opinion, the countryfolk have always loved their masters. Both they and we have a proper self-respect and know our places. It is in the ranks of the lower middle class that you find social hatred, and it springs from envy. It was the middle classes that did most of the butchering during the Terror. . . ."

Her daughter-in-law declared in self-complacent tones that, owing to the treachery of the emigrés, the Terror had been "just and necessary". At that, the Baronne drew herself majestically to her full height.

"My great-grandfather, and two of my great-uncles perished on the scaffold, and I forbid you . . . ."

Paula suddenly found herself thinking of the schoolmaster. Her words would have pleased him. He would have approved her attitude. Paula's views had been inherited from her Meulière uncle, a narrowly fanatical Radical and Freemason. But her expression of them took on a special value for her now that she was offering them on the altar of the man she was to see to-morrow. It was Thursday, and he would be free. What she had said, had been said as a result of *his* influence (uncle Meulière had had nothing to do with it), the influence of someone to whom she had never spoken, whom she had seen occasionally in the street, who never so much as said "Good Morning" if she happened to pass when he was working in his garden (though he would pause in his digging to look at her).

"Do you know what you are, my dear? – an incendiary: nothing more nor less than an incendiary. . . ."

Guillaume raised his head. He knew what an incendiary was. Hundreds of times he had looked at a picture in the 1871 volume of *Le Monde Illustré*, which showed two women squatting in the darkness by a cellar door, making some sort of a fire. Locks of untidy hair straggled from underneath their proletarian caps. . . . He gazed at his mother with his mouth open . . . an incendiary? – why, of course she was! . . .

She grabbed him by the arm.

"Upstairs with you – quick now!"

The Baronne made the sign of the cross upon his forehead with her thumb: but she did not kiss him. As soon as he had left the room, she said:

"We ought at least to spare him. . . ."

"You needn't worry, he doesn't hear, and if he did hear, he wouldn't understand."

"That is where you are wrong. Poor little mite! He

understands a great deal more than we think. . . . And, talking of him brings me back to the subject of our discussion, We seem to have strayed a long way from it, and for that we are equally to blame. If, as I have very little doubt, and, as I hope, will be the case, this man persists in his refusal. . . ."

"In that case, there'll be nothing for it but to let Guillaume grow up like a little country lout. . . . It's nothing short of a shame to see rich people's children enjoying all the benefits of an education from which they are incapable of profiting, while those of the poor . . . ."

Once again, the commonplaces which had been constantly in uncle Meulière's mouth went suddenly to her head. No doubt her views would be shared by the schoolmaster, whom she credited with every kind of advanced theory. It never occurred to her that he might not be built to the official pattern.

The old lady, determined to avoid a fresh outburst, got up without saying a word. Paula followed her to the stairs.

"Why should not you and I join forces and teach him what little we know?"

"If you've got sufficient patience, well and good. I confess that I've had about as much as I can stand."

"A good night's sleep will work wonders, my dear.

Please forget anything I have said that may have wounded you, as I, for my part, freely forgive you."

Her daughter-in-law indulged in a shrug: "That's just so much talk, and doesn't really alter what we feel. We can no longer have any illusions. . . ."

They stood facing one another in the bedroom corridor, candle in hand. Of the two faces thus brightly illuminated, that of the younger woman looked by far the most formidable.

"Please believe, Paula, that I am a great deal less unfair in my attitude than you, quite naturally think. You have much to excuse you . . . the burden you have been called upon to bear is heavy for a young woman . . . ."

"I was twenty-six" broke in Paula sharply. "I blame nobody. My fate was of my own choosing. If it comes to that, you, poor thing. . . ."

The meaning behind her words was – my wretched husband is your wretched son. She found some consolation for the hell in which she lived in the knowledge that she shared it with her old enemy. But the Baronne refused the proffered sympathy.

"With me it is quite different," she replied in a voice shaken by emotion. "I, after all, had my Adhémar. For twenty-five years I was the happiest of women. . . ."

"Perhaps . . . but not the happiest of mothers."

"It is five years since my Georges died a hero's death.

I do not weep for him. I still have his little Danièle, I still have Galéas . . . ."

"Yes, you most certainly have Galéas!"

"I have my children in Paris" – went on the other obstinately.

"But they just sponge on you. For them you have never been anything but a cow to be milked. You may shake your head as much as you like, but you know it as well as I do. Fraûlein throws it in your teeth often enough when the two of you are alone and think that I am out of hearing. . . . No, let me go on . . . I *will* raise my voice if I want to . . . ."

The words, echoing down the corridor, woke Guillaume with a start. He sat up in bed. The gods were still hard at it up there in the sky. He snuggled down again, a pillow pressed against one ear, his finger stuck in the other. While he lay there waiting for sleep to come again, he took up the thread of the story he had been telling himself, about the island and the cave – like in *Un Robinson de douze ans*. The night-light peopled the linen-closet in which he slept with familiar shadows and with monsters tamed.

"We live here deprived of everything so that your Arbis daughter may keep her state in Paris, and weave what she calls her marriage plots. What does it matter if we starve so long as Yolande marries a Duke with

Jewish blood, and Stanislas an American nobody...."

Thus did Paula nag away at the old lady who, eager for silence, retreated hurriedly and bolted her door. But through the panels the implacable voice still sounded.

"The fewer hopes you have of Stanislas, the better. *He'll* never marry anybody, that little ...."

She finished up with a word the meaning of which the Baronne would not have grasped even if she had heard it, even if she had not been kneeling at her prie-Dieu with her head buried in her arms.

No sooner had Paula shut herself into her own room than her anger fell dead. There were still a few embers glowing in the grate. She threw on a fresh log, lit the oil-lamp on the table by the sofa, undressed in front of the fire, and put on an old quilted dressing-gown ....

We speak of "making love": we should be able, too, to speak of "making hate". To make hate is comforting. It rests the mind and relaxes the nerves. Paula opened the wardrobe. Her hands hovered, momentarily hesitating. Then she chose the curaçao, pitched the sofa cushions on-to the floor, as near the fire as possible, and stretched herself out at full length with a glass and a bottle within easy reach of her hand. She started to smoke and to drink, thinking the while of the man, of the schoolmaster, who was the enemy of all aristocrats and rich folk, a "red", maybe, a Communist. He was despised as she was despised, and by the same type of person. Before him she would humble herself, and, in the end, would force her way into his life. He was married . . . what was his wife like? She did not even know her by sight. For the time being she kept her strictly out of the story she was imagining, burrowing into her fantasy, prodigal of more invention that ever professional story-teller showed. Before her inner eye visions arose beyond the power of language to express. Now and again she got to her feet to put another log upon the fire and to fill her glass. Then she lay down again. The occasional flicker of a flame played on her face, revealing the mask of now a criminal – now a martyr.

CHAPTER II

II

EARLY next afternoon, wearing a mackintosh, heavy shoes, and a beret pulled down over her eyes, she made her way to the village. The rain beating on her face, she thought, would wash away the tell-tale signs of last night's orgy. She no longer felt exalted. Only determination kept her going. Any other woman would have spent hours choosing what clothes she should put on for so important a mission, or, if not that, would at least have tried to look her best. It never so much as occurred to Paula to powder her face, or to do anything that would make the hirsute appearance of her cheeks less noticeable. If only she had washed her hair it might have looked less greasy. It should have entered her mind that the schoolmaster might, like most other men, be susceptible to scent. But no: without paying any more attention than usual to her person, and looking as bedraggled as always, she set out to try her luck for the last time.

The man, the schoolmaster, was sitting in the kitchen, facing his wife. He was shelling kidney-beans, and chatting as he worked. . . . It was Thursday, the best day of the whole week. The schoolhouse faced the street, like all the other houses of the ugly village of Cernès. The smithy, the butcher's shop, the inn and the post-office were not, as elsewhere, grouped about the church, which, set in solitude among its huddle of graves, stood upon a promontory, dominating the valley of the Ciron. . . . Cernès had only one street, and even that was not a street proper, but only the main-road. The school-house stood a little way back from it. The children used the front door, and the schoolmaster's kitchen opened off to the right of the narrow passage which led to the play-ground, and, beyond it, to the kitchen-garden. Robert and Léone Bordas, untouched by any presentiment of the fate which was approaching their home, were once again hard at it discussing their strange visitor of the day before.

"It's all very well your talking", his wife was saying with no little eagerness, "but a hundred and fifty, perhaps two hundred francs extra each month, just for seeing that the kid from the great house keeps his nose to the grindstone, are not to be sneezed at. Anyway, it's worth thinking about."

"We haven't sunk that far. There's nothing, I can see, that we have to do without. I'm getting practically all the books I want now . . ." (he did the reviewing of poetry and fiction for the *Teachers' Journal*).

"You never think about anybody but yourself. After all, there's Jean-Pierre to be considered. . . ."

"Jean-Pierre's got all he needs. You're not suggesting, I suppose, that he should have a coach?"

Her smile expressed satisfaction. No, certainly, their boy didn't need anything of that kind. He was always top of his class in every subject. Though he was only thirteen, he had just got into the Upper School a good two years ahead of the normal time, and would almost certainly have to stay in it an extra three terms, because it was very unlikely that his age would be taken into account. He was already being picked for a winner at the Lycée, and his masters had very little doubt that he would pass the School Certificate at the first attempt, both in Science and the Humanities.

"That's where you're wrong: I do want him to take private lessons."

As Léone made this announcement there was nothing in the expression of her face to indicate either that she had any doubts of her own wisdom, or that she felt she was asking a favour. She was a thin, pale woman with reddish hair and small features. Though not in her first youth, she was still pretty. Her voice was rather sharp and penetrating as a result of having to keep a roomful of youngsters in order.

"He must learn riding."

Robert Bordas went on with his task of shelling beans. He affected to believe that she was joking.

"Of course he must, and dancing too, I suppose, if you want him to."

Laughter creased his long and rather narrow eyes. He was wearing no collar and was unshaven. Nevertheless, there was something still of the charm of youth about him. It was easy to see what he must have been like as a boy. He got up and moved round the table, leaning on a cane with a rubber ferule. He limped, but only very slightly. His long, supple cat's back was that of an adolescent. He lit a cigarette and said:

"I know somebody who longs for the Revolution – but wants a racing-stable for her son!"

She shrugged her shoulders.

"Why do you want to turn Jean-Pierre into a horseman" – he would not let the subject drop – "So's he can serve in the Dragoons with a lot of rotters who'll send the schoolmaster's son to Coventry?"

"Don't get excited. You'd better take care of your voice. You'll need it at the 11th November Meeting. . . ."

She saw from his face that she had gone too far, emptied her apronful of beans into a dish, and gave her husband a kiss. "Listen to me, Robert. . . ." She wanted the same things as he wanted. He knew that. She followed him blindly and with utter confidence. Politics were not for her. She found it difficult to imagine how the world would go once the Revolution was an accomplished fact. The only thing she knew for certain was that there would always be an élite who would rule the country. It would be drawn, of course, from the most intelligent and the best educated, but also from those with the gift of leadership.

"All right then, I do want Jean-Pierre to know how to ride a horse, and, more than anything, I want him to acquire those virtues of initiative, courage and enterprise in which he is rather lacking. He's got everything else, but not them."

Robert Bordas looked at the absent expression on his wife's face. She was completely unaware of him. Her heart, at that moment, was far away.

"The Ecole Normale trains an élite of University teachers" – he observed with a touch of dryness. "That is the sole purpose of its existence."

"But think of all the Ministers, all the great writers, all the Party chiefs, who have passed through it: Jaurès, first and foremost, Léon Blum...."

He broke in on her.

"Personally speaking, I should be quite proud enough if Jean-Pierre could produce a first-rate thesis, and end up as a Professor in the Faculty of Letters. I ask nothing better for him ... or even, perhaps, at the Sorbonne, or, who knows ... at the Collège de France!"

There was a touch of bitterness in her laughter.

"It's my turn now to point out what a fine revolutionary *you* make! Do you really imagine that all those antiques will be left standing?"

"Of course they will! The University will be transformed, no doubt, and injected with new blood. But in France, higher education will always be higher education. . . . You don't know what you're talking about. . . ."

Suddenly he stopped speaking. He had just seen, through the glazed panel of the door, the figure of a woman emerging from the mist.

"Who on earth is that?"

"Some mother, I expect, who has come to complain that her darling is being treated unfairly."

Paula took a long time scraping her boots and ridding them of mud before she entered the house. They did not recognize her. They had no idea who this strange woman could be, with a beret pulled down over dark, black-circled eyes, and a face which had as thick a growth of down as a youth's. She carefully avoided mentioning her name. All she said to Robert was that she was the mother of the boy about whom the Baronne de Cernès had spoken to him on the previous day. It took him a few seconds to grasp the significance of her words, but Léone had already guessed.

She led the way into a freezingly cold room, and

threw open the shutters. Everything was bright and shining, the floor, the sideboard and the table in department-store style. A coarse lace blind masked the window. There was a wide frieze with a design of giant hydrangeas just below the ceiling. The wall paper was dark red.

"I will leave you with my husband...."

Paula protested that she had no secrets to discuss. It was just a question of clearing up a slight misunderstanding. Robert Bordas's cheeks had flushed a bright red. They had always done that ever since he was a child. His ears were aflame. Was this woman with the evil gleam in her eye going to make him give an account of his yesterday's half-joking behaviour? Indeed she was! – she had the brazen effrontery to embark at once on the subject, without the slightest show of embarrassment. She was afraid, she said, that her mother-in-law had misunderstood some perfectly innocent remark of his, and had gone off in a huff. She had no intention of asking Monsieur Bordas to withdraw his refusal, but she would hate to think that the incident had created a new enemy for herself in the village. She was so defenceless, and he was one of the few persons from whom she had the right to expect some measure of understanding.

She turned her blazing eyes from Robert to Léone. The slightly drooping corners of her mouth gave the look of a tragic mask to the great hairy face. Robert stammered that he was deeply shocked, that there had been no intention of offence in what he had said. Paula cut him short, and, turning to Léone:

"I never thought there had been," – she said. "You have only too good reason to know, both of you, what the people round here are like, and how they gossip."

Had they understood the veiled allusion? Had they heard the story which was going round to the effect that the schoolmaster had been wounded whilst holding a cushy job in one of the back-areas? Some went so far as to hint that he had let off his own rifle . . . pure clumsiness, of course, but. . . .

They showed no sign of embarrassment. Paula had no idea whether she had touched them on the raw or not.

She went on:

"I know, madame, that you come of an old Cadillac family. . . ."

It was, indeed, true that Léone's parents were peasant-proprietors in a small way, and belonged to an honourable and ancient line. But they had been looked at askance because of their advanced views. Their daughter had not had a church wedding, and there seemed to be some doubt as to whether Jean-Pierre had been baptized. In order to stay near the family, the Bordas had given up a chance of rapid promotion.

"Cernès", said Paula, "has a better schoolmaster than it deserves."

Once again the young face opposite flushed crimson. But there was no stopping her. She knew, she said, that Robert Bordas had only to raise a finger to be a Deputy to-morrow if he chose.

His colour deepened, but he merely shrugged his shoulders:

"You're pulling my leg!"

Léone laughed:

"You'll be turning my poor Robert's head, madame!"

The young man's face creased in a smile. "I'm not expressing my own views. It was Monsieur Lousteau, our bailiff, who said that. He's a friend of yours, I believe? Of course, he's a Royalist, but he can be fair to his enemies. With a husband like your's, madame, a woman can afford to be ambitious."

In a low voice, she added: "If I were in your shoes!..." The tone in which she said this was exactly right. There was no undue stressing of the allusion to her own wretched husband.

"Jean-Pierre will be the first great man in *our* family" – said the schoolmaster with a laugh: "isn't that so, Léone?"

Their son? The visitor's smile expressed understanding. His name had reached even her ears. Monsieur Lousteau had often spoken of him. How happy they must be, and how proud! Again she sighed, again she showed that her own misfortune was uppermost in her mind. But this time she made no bones about talking of it.

"Speaking of infant prodigies, reminds me. It was to discuss the future of my own son that I came here to-day I think it not unlikely that my mother-in-law may have slightly exaggerated the position. He *is* backward, I know, and I realize that the suggestion she made may rather have frightened you!"

Robert protested vigorously that lack of leisure, and the dread of not being able to devote enough time to an additional job, had alone prompted his refusal. His duties as Mayor's secretary, and his own private work, took up every moment he could spare from his teaching.

"Oh, I know what a worker you are!" – she said, adding in a sly tone of flattery: "a little bird has been whispering that certain unsigned articles in *la France du Sud-Ouest....*"

Once again, the schoolmaster's cheeks and ears glowed scarlet. In order to cut the interview short, he began to put a few questions to her about Guillaume. Could the boy read and write fluently? He actually read sometimes for pleasure, did he? – well, then, he certainly was not a hopeless case.

Paula felt a little uncertain how to proceed.

It was important not to put this man off at the start. All the same, it was only wise to make him realize what a little half-wit his future pupil was. Yes, she said, there were two or three books which he read over and over again, and he was for ever browsing over bound numbers of the *Saint-Nicholas Annual* dating from the 'nineties, though there was no reason to think that he took anything in. She was afraid her little "brat" was not very attractive, not very winning. One had to be his mother before one could put up with him at all, and there were times when even she. . . . The schoolmaster felt his heart bleed for her. The best thing, he suggested, would be for him to have the boy round after five o'clock one evening, when school was over, just to see what he was like. He would not make any definite promise until he had had an opportunity to study him.

Paula took both his hands in hers. Emotion, only half feigned, made her voice tremble as she said:

"I can't help thinking of the difference you will find between my poor, unhappy boy and your own son!"

She turned away her face as though to keep him from seeing how ashamed she felt. . . . Her behaviour, this afternoon, had been nothing short of inspired! Something undreamed of had happened to this teacher and his schoolmarm wife. They had grown used to living in an atmosphere of perpetual hostility, of being objects of suspicion to countryfolk and gentry alike, of being treated by the clergy as public enemies – and now, someone from the great house had come to ask a favour of them! Just fancy what it must mean to them to know that she not only admired, but actually envied, them! In how humble a tone had she referred to her own husband and her degenerate son! . . . The adventure had quite gone to Robert's head. He could not forget that this beret and this mackintosh concealed a genuine lady of title! He could not resist a little mild badinage.

"I find it a little surprising, madame, that you should not be afraid of my influence on the boy. . . . My views, you know, are not at all what is usually called respectable."

Again the creases appeared in his face. His eyes almost vanished, so that only their glitter showed between the half-closed lids.

"You don't know me" replied Paula with a serious air – "or what I am really like."

If she told them that nothing would please her more than to think her poor boy capable of responding to that influence, they would not believe her.

"The world in which I live is not my world. I am just as much a fish out of water as you would be . . . one of these days I'll tell you. . . ."

In this way did she prepare the way for future confidences. No need to say more: no need to break down barriers. She would say good-bye now, for the time being, leaving them quite overwhelmed by what she had just said about her "views". . . . It was agreed that she should bring Guillaume to the schoolhouse next afternoon, about four. Then, all of a sudden, she became the great lady, the replica of her mother-in-law, of the Comtesse d'Arbis.

"So many thanks! You have no idea how relieved I feel. Yes, really, I mean it. Our little chat has meant *so* much to me."

"It's pretty obvious she's fallen for you" said Léone.

She had cleared the table, and now, with a sigh, took up a number of exercises which she had got to correct.

"She's not a bad sort, you know."

"There you are! She was very careful to treat you with respect, but, if you want my opinion, you'd better watch your step!"

"She's a bit touched, I should say . . . or, to put it mildly, rather hysterical."

"She knows what she wants all right, touched or not. Don't forget that story about her and the curé! I think you ought to go very carefully."

He got up, stretched his long arms, and said:

"I don't like bearded ladies."

"She wouldn't be bad looking", said Léone ,"if she took more care of herself.'

"I remember now what Lousteau told me. She's not an aristocrat by birth, but the daughter, or niece, of Meulière who was once Mayor of Bordeaux. . . . Why are you laughing?"

"Her not being a genuine aristocrat seems to depress you!"

While his mother was making ready to hand him over to the tender mercies of the red schoolmaster, the poor little hare, hunted from his form, was wondering whether he would ever get back to it. The bright light of the grown-up world into which he had been chased made him blink. During his mother's absence, a difference of opinion had developed between his three beneficent deities – Papa, Mamie and Fraülein. Mamie and Fraülein, it is true, were frequently at loggerheads, but almost always about things which didn't much matter. The Austrian woman would sometimes employ language which seemed the cruder for being couched in the respectful third person. But to-day Guillaume had an uncomfortable feeling that even Fraûlein was in favour of his being entrusted to the schoolmaster.

"Why should he not have a proper education? he's as good as anybody else!"

Then, turning to him:

"Run away and play, my duckie, my chickabiddy. . . ."

He left the house, but, a moment later, came back and slipped into the kitchen. Wasn't it the general view that he never listened, and that, even if he did, he couldn't understand?

The Baronne, without condescending to answer Fraûlein, was haranguing her son, who was lolling in his favourite wicker armchair in front of the kitchen fire. He spent almost every rainy afternoon of Winter there, making paper spills, or polishing his father's guns, which he never used.

"Do exert a little authority, for once in your life, Galéas!" – the old lady was saying. "You've only got to say 'No, I won't have my son handed over to this Communist!' ... There'll be a storm, of course, but it'll blow over."

Fraûlein entered a protest:

"Don't you listen to Madame la Baronne" (having nursed Galéas as a baby, she habitually addressed him in the singular). "Why should not Guillou be as well educated as the Arbis children?"

"You leave the Arbis children alone, Fraûlein. This has got nothing to do with them. I don't wish my grandson to be inculcated with this man's ideas – that's the long and the short of it."

"Poor chick! – as though anyone was going to talk politics to him!"

"It is not a question of politics. . . . There is religion to be considered. The boy's not so strong in his catechism as he might be. . . ."

Guillaume watched his father sitting there without stirring a finger. He was staring at the smouldering logs, and showed no sign of inclining to one side or other of the argument. Guillou, his mouth half open, was trying hard to understand.

"Madame la Baronne does not really mind him living like a clodhopper when he's grown up . . . for all I know, she may prefer to have it that way!"

"The idea of you setting yourself up against me and pleading my grandson's cause! That really is too much!" – The Baronne tried to sound indignant, but it was clear that she did not feel very sure of herself.

"Oh, I know that Madame la Baronne is very fond of Guillou, and likes having him with her here: but it is not him she has in mind when she thinks about the future of the family."

The Baronne professed to regard Fraûlein as a bull in a china shop. But the Austrian's shrill voice easily drowned her mistress's.

"And the proof of that, if proof were needed, is that after Georges' death, it was agreed that Stanislas, the eldest Arbis boy, should add the name Cernès to his own, as though there were no other Cernès left, as though Guillou wasn't really Guillaume de Cernès."

"The boy's listening", said Galéas suddenly, and then relapsed once more into silence. Fraûlein took Guillou by the shoulders and gently pushed him through the door. But he went no further than the pantry, where Fraûlein's loud tones reached him easily.

"I know somebody who wasn't called 'Desiré' when he turned up. Madame la Baronne will doubtless remember her own words – that it couldn't be a very common occurrence for an invalid to get a child on his sicknurse...."

"I never said any such thing, Fraûlein! ... Galéas was perfectly well and strong.... Besides, it is not my custom to make coarse remarks of that kind."

"Madame la Baronne will surely recollect that a child was no part of the bargain. I, who knew my Galéas, was well aware that he was as good as the next man – as the event proved...."

A dangerous glitter showed between the Austrian's reddish, lashless lids – "pig's eyes" – Madame Galéas had once called them. The Baronne, shocked by what had just been said, turned away.

Guillaume, his nose pressed to the pantry window, was watching the splashing raindrops. They looked like little dancing figures. The grown-ups seemed to be for ever going on about him, and quarrelling, too. No one had found it possible to call him "Desiré". He wanted to go on telling himself the stories which only he knew. But this time there would be no excuse, unless the schoolmaster went on refusing. If he did that, Guillou would be so happy that he wouldn't a bit mind not being called "Desiré". All he asked was not to have to be with a lot of other children who would make his life a misery to him, not to have anything to do with schoolmasters with their loud voices, their bad tempers, their stern looks, and the way they had of producing a lot of words which didn't mean anything.

Mamie hadn't wanted him, nor his own mother neither. He knew that all right. Had they foreseen that he wouldn't be like other boys? How about poor Papa? – had *he* wanted him? He didn't know, but he did know that Papa wouldn't be any good at getting him out of the schoolmaster's clutches.

The Baronne was keeping on at that very subject, until she was sick of the sound of her own voice.

"You've only got to say 'no' – surely it's not all that difficult! Listen to me, it's just a question of saying 'no'. . . . Since you've only got to say 'no'. . . ."

But all he did was to sit there shaking his great mop of grizzled hair, and saying nothing. Finally, however, he did speak:

"I haven't the right. . . ."

"Haven't the right? what do you mean, Galéas? Who, then, has a right if not the father of a family, where his children's education is concerned?"

But he kept on shaking his head, looking mulish, and repeating:

"I haven't the right. . . ."

It was then that Guillaume ran back into the room in tears, and flung himself into Fraûlein's lap.

"Here's mummy! – and she's laughing to herself: oh! I know it means that the schoolmaster's going to. . . ."

"What of it – you little silly? He won't eat you! Wipe his nose, Fraülein, he's a disgusting sight."

He vanished into the scullery, just as his mother entered the kitchen with a look of triumph on her face.

"It's all arranged," she said: "I'm to take Guillaume along there to-morrow afternoon at four."

"If your husband is agreeable."

"Oh naturally: but he'll be agreeable all right, won't you, Galéas?"

"You're going to have your work cut out with that boy, whatever you do. . . ."

"That reminds me – where is he?" asked Paula: "I thought I heard him snuffling."

They caught sight of Guillaume sneaking out of the scullery. He was looking his very worst, with tears, and dribble and snot all over his face.

"I won't go!" he whined, without looking at his mother. "I won't go to the schoolmaster!"

Paula had always been ashamed of him, but now, behind the boy's puckered face was the image of the father in his chair. The child's drooling mouth was the very replica of that other mouth, moist, and without warmth.

With an effort she controlled her temper. In a voice that was almost gentle she said:

"Of course, I can't drag you there by force. But, if you won't go, you'll have to be sent away to board at the Lycée."

The Baronne shrugged her shoulders. "You know perfectly well that no school would keep such a little misery."

"Then I see nothing for it but a Reformatory. . . ."

She had uttered this particular threat so often that Guillaume had ended by conjuring up a vague but terrifying image of those disciplinary establishments. He began to tremble. "No! mummy, no!" he blubbered, and, hurling himself into Fraûlein's arms, hid his face against her flabby bosom.

"Don't you believe a word she says, my chick. You don't think I'd let her do a thing like that, do you?"

"Fraûlein has no say in the matter. And this time I'm not joking. I have made enquiries, and have several addresses" – said Paula, and there was a note of gay excitement in her voice.

What finally brought him to the breaking point was the sound of old Mamie's laughter.

"Why not just put him in a sack, my dear, and have done with it? Why not throw him into the river like a kitten?"

Mad with terror, he began scrubbing away at his face with a filthy handkerchief.

"Oh, no, Mamie, no! – not in a sack!"

Irony meant nothing to him. Everything he heard he took quite literally.

"Little silly!" said the Baronne, and drew him to her, but only to push him away again, quite gently.

"Really, it is difficult to know what to do for the best. Such a grubby little urchin – take him, Fraülein . . . run away, my boy, and clean yourself."

His teeth were chattering: "I *will* go to the schoolmaster, mummy; I *will* be good! . . ."

"Ah, now you're seeing sense at last!"

Fraülein took him along to the scullery, and washed his face at the tap.

"They only want to frighten you, my chick. They don't mean what they say: just you laugh at them!"

At this point Galéas got out of his chair, and, without a glance at any of them, said:

"It's quite fine now. You coming along to the churchyard, son?"

Guillou dreaded going for walks with his father, but this time, he gladly took the proffered hand, and started off, still snuffling.

It had stopped raining, and the drenched grass was sparkling in the warm sunlight. They walked along a field-path which skirted the village. Ordinarily, Guillaume was afraid of cows, of the way they raised their heads and stared, as though they were making up their minds to charge. His father had tight hold of his hand, and said nothing. They could have walked for hours without exchanging a word. Guillou could not know that these silences were his father's despair, that the poor man was trying, all the while, to concentrate his mind. But he could not think of anything to say to a small boy.

They entered the churchyard through a hole in the wall, choked with nettles. It lay at the east end of the building.

The graves were still covered with the faded remnants of flowers laid there on All Saints' Day. Galéas dropped his son's hand, and went in search of a barrow. Guillou watched him walk away. That was his father – that darned brown jersey, those trouser legs which looked as though there were nothing inside them, that tousled head under the tiny beret. He waited for him, seated on a gravestone which was half buried in the grass. The late sun had warmed it slightly. All the same, he felt cold. The thought came to him that he might catch a chill, that he might not be able to leave the house to-morrow. To die . . . to become like the people he tried to imagine lying under this rich soil – the dead, those human moles, marking their presence with little heaps of earth.

Beyond the wall he could see the countryside already emptied of life by the approach of Winter: the shivering vines, the greasy, sticky soil – an element at odds with man, to which it would be as mad to trust oneself as to the waves of the sea. At the bottom of the slope the Ciron flowed on towards the river, a small stream, swollen by the rains, moving through mysterious marshlands and a tangled wilderness of water-plants. Guillou had heard the villagers say that sometimes they had put up woodcock there. Like one of them, the boy, driven from his hiding-place, sat trembling with cold and fear, with nothing to protect him from a hostile world and nature's cruelty. On the hillside, the industrial red of brand-new roofs shone harshly. Instinctively, his eyes sought the rain-worn pink of old and round-backed tiles. Close at hand, the church wall showed dishonourable cracks. One of the coloured windows had been broken. He knew that "the Good God was not there", that the curé would not leave God in such a place for fear of sacrilege. Nor was the Good God in their Chapel at home, which Fraülein used now as a room in which to keep brooms and packing-cases and broken chairs. Where in this harsh world had God set up His dwelling? Where was a trace of Him to be found?

Guillou felt cold. A nettle had stung him on the calf. He got up and walked the few paces which lay between him and the War Memorial, unveiled the year before. There were thirteen names for this one small village: De Cernès, Georges; Laclotte, Jean; Lapeyre, Joseph; Lapeyre, Ernest; Lartigue, René; . . . Guillaume saw between the gravestones his father's brown jersey bend down, then straighten, and heard the squeaking of the barrow wheels. To-morrow he was to be handed over to the red schoolmaster. Perhaps the schoolmaster would die suddenly in the night. Something might happen – a hurricane, an earthquake. . . . But nothing would ever silence his mother's terrible voice, nothing would ever put out the terrible gleam in her eyes which, when they rested on him, made him conscious, all at once, of his skinniness, of his dirty knees, of his wrinkled and untidy socks. On those occasions, Guillaume would swallow his saliva, and, in the hope of pacifying the enemy, shut his mouth. . . . But the exasperated voice shattered the silence (it was as though it had pursued him into the tiny graveyard where he stood shivering) – "Oh, go away, do: anywhere you like, so long as I don't see you!"

About the same time, Paula had lit the fire in her bedroom, and was giving free play to her thoughts. No one can make themselves beloved at will, or attract another merely by wishing to. But no power in Heaven, or in the earth beneath, can keep a woman from picking out one man from the crowd, and choosing him to be her god. It does not matter to him, since he is not asked to give anything in return. It is she who decides to make him the idol at the centre of her life. There is nothing she can do but raise an altar in the desert, and consecrate it to her curly-headed divinity.

Others, in the end, always ask favours of their god, but she was determined to ask nothing of hers. She would rob him only of what can be taken from another without his knowledge. . . . How miraculous a power dwells in the furtive glance, in the undisciplined thought! A day might come perhaps when she would dare to make some gesture of approach, and then – who knows? – her god might bear, without flinching, the touch of lips upon his hand.

CHAPTER III

III

HURRIEDLY, his mother dragged him along the road. The ruts were filled with rain-water. They passed the children going home from school, who spoke no word, nor laughed. The satchels on their backs were only to be guessed at from the way they showed as humps beneath the capes. Dark eyes and light from all these little hunchbacks gleamed from the shadow of their hoods. Guillou thought how soon they would have grown to be tormentors had he been forced to work and play with them. But he was to be delivered, sole and unaccompanied, to the schoolmaster who would have no one else to occupy his mind, who would concentrate upon his single person that terrifying power all grown-ups had to crush him with their questions, to weigh upon him with their arguments and explanations. No longer would that power be spread over a whole classroom of children. Guillou, and Guillou alone, would have to stand up to this monster of knowledge, who would be exasperated, irritated, by the presence of a boy who could not even understand the words with which his ears were being deafened.

He was going to school at a time when the other pupils

were on their way home. The thought that that was so made a deep impression on him. He felt different, he felt lonely. The dry, warm hand which held his own tightened its grip. A force that was indifferent, if not actually hostile, to his feelings, was dragging him along. Shut away in a secret world of passions and of thoughts, his mother spoke not a single word. Already they had reached the first houses of the village. The lamps and the firelight shining behind the clouded window panes, cast a radiance on the dusk. The smoke of chimneys filled the night air with a smell of burning. From the Hotel Dupuy there streamed a brighter glow. Two waggons were standing in front of the door. The broad backs of their drivers were jostling before the bar. Still a minute to go. The light over there—*that* was it. He remembered the gruff voice his grandmother put on when she told him the tale of *Tom Thumb* – "*It was the ogre's house*". Through the glass panes of the front door he could see the ogre's wife on the look out for her prey.

"What are you trembling for, you little fool? Monsieur Bordas won't eat you."

" Perhaps he's cold?"

Paula shrugged, and said irritably:

"No, it's just nerves. It always takes him like that, for no apparent reason. He suffered from convulsions when he was eighteen months old."

Guillou's teeth were chattering. The only sound to be heard was the noise they made, and the ticking of the grandfather clock.

"Take off his boots, Léone," said the ogre, "and give him Jean-Pierre's slippers."

"Oh, please," protested Paula, "don't go to all that trouble."

But already Léone was coming back into the room with a pair of slippers. She perched Guillou on her knee, took off his cape, and moved close to the fire.

"Aren't you ashamed, a great big boy like you?" – said his mother. "I haven't brought any of his school-books or notebooks with me," she added.

The ogre assured her that he did not need them. This evening they would just talk and get to know each other.

"I'll come back in two hours," said Paula. Guillou could not hear what his mother and the schoolmaster were whispering in the entry. He knew that she had gone because he no longer felt cold. The front door had been shut.

"Would you like to help us shell kidney-beans?" Léone asked. "But perhaps you don't know how?"

He laughed and said that he always helped Fraülein. This talk of beans gave him a sense of security. He plucked up courage to add: "Ours have been picked for a long time."

"These," said the schoolmaster's wife, "are the late kind. A lot of them are bad; you'll have to sort them out."

Guillou drew up to the table and started on the work. The Bordas's kitchen was very like every other kitchen. It had a wide hearth with a pot hanging from a hook, a long table, copper saucepans on a dresser, a row of jam jars on another, and two hams in sacks suspended from the beams. . . . But Guillou felt that he had come into a strange, delicious world. Was it the smell of the pipe which was always in Monsieur Bordas's mouth even when it wasn't alight? What most struck him were the books everywhere, and the piles of magazines on the sideboard, and on a small table which stood within easy reach of the schoolmaster's hand. He sat there now, with his legs stretched out, paying no attention to Guillou, but engaged in cutting the pages of a Review which had a white cover with the title printed in red.

Above the chimney-piece was the portrait of a big, bearded man with folded arms. There was a word printed beneath it which the boy tried to spell out in a low voice from where he was sitting: "Jaur . . . Jau. . . ."

"Jaurès," said the ogre suddenly: "do you know who Jaurès was?"

Guillou shook his head. Léone broke in: "Surely you're not going to start by talking to him about Jaurès?"

"He began it" – said Monsieur Bourdas. He laughed. Guillou liked his eyes when they were all squinnied up with laughter. He would have liked to know who Jaurès was. He didn't at all mind shelling kidney-beans. He made a separate pile of the bad ones. He was being left to himself. He could think his own thoughts and take in the ogre, the ogre's wife and their house.

"Had enough of it?" Monsieur Bordas asked suddenly.

He was not reading his Review. He glanced through the table of contents, cut the pages, paused now and again at the names of the various contributors, held the paper close to his face, sniffing at it greedily. A magazine straight from Paris. He thought how unbelievably happy must be the lives of the men who worked on it. He tried to picture their faces, the Editor's room where they met to exchange views . . . men, all of them, who knew everything, who had made the "circuit of the human mind". . . . Léone did not know that he had sent in an essay he had written on Romains Rolland. It had been refused, though the letter that told him so had been extremely polite. His approach had been too markedly political. The rain was now splashing on the roof and gurgling in the gutters. One has only one life, and Robert Bordas would never know what it was like to live in Paris. Monsieur Lousteau was for ever telling him that he could write a book about his experiences at Cernès, and advising him to keep a Journal. But he wasn't interested in himself. He wasn't, if it came to that, very much interested in other people either. He would have liked to persuade them, impose his ideas on them, but as individuals they did not appeal to him. . . . He had the gift of words, of writing articles at short notice. Monsieur Lousteau thought his contributions to *la France du Sud-Ouest* better than anything published in Paris, except in *l'Action française*. There was no one on the staff of *l'Humanité*, so Lousteau said, to hold a candle to him. . . . Paris. . . . He had promised Léone never to leave Cernès, not even when Jean-Pierre went to the Ecole Normale . . . not even later, when their son should have made his mark, and was occupying a high position. He mustn't be an old man of the sea, mustn't get in the lad's way. "Everyone's got his own place in life," said Léone.

Robert got up and stood for a while with his face pressed to the glass panel of the front door. Coming back into the room, he saw Guillou's moist and gentle eyes fixed upon him. The boy looked away as he approached, and the schoolmaster remembered that he liked reading.

"Had enough of shelling beans, old man? Like me to lend you a picture-book?"

Guillou replied that it wouldn't matter if there weren't any pictures.

"Show him Jean-Pierre's library," said Léone, "then he can choose for himself."

Monsieur Bordas, carrying a paraffin lamp, led the way into the family bedroom. To the boy, following him, it seemed magnificent. The huge carved bedstead was dominated by a cherry-coloured eiderdown. It was as though red-current syrup had been spilled all over the counterpane. A number of enlarged photographs hung on the walls, close to the ceiling. Monsieur Bordas introduced him into a smaller room which had a slightly stuffy smell. It seemed to have been shut up for some time. The schoolmaster proudly raised the lamp, and, at once, Guillou was lost in admiration of Bordas Junior's room.

"Not so fine as up at the big-house, of course," said his guide: "still," he added, with a self-satisfied air, "it's not too bad. . . ."

The boy could scarcely believe his eyes. For the first time this little scion of a noble line found himself thinking of the hole in which he spent his nights. It was impregnated with the smell of Mademoiselle Adrienne who was in charge of the household linen, and spent all her afternoons there. A dressmaker's dummy, now out of use, stood beside a sewing-machine, and there was a truckle bed covered with a dustsheet, which Fraûlein occupied when Guillou was ill. He had a sudden vision of the shabby piece of rug on which he had so often upset his chamber-pot. This room was all Jean-Pierre's own, with its painted bed in blue and white, and its glass-fronted, well-stocked bookcase.

" Almost all the volumes are prizes," said Monsieur Bordas. "He's always top of his form."

Guillou touched each separate book with loving fingers.

" Take what you'd like."

" Oh! . . . *The Mysterious Island !* . . . have you read that?" – he asked, looking at Monsieur Bordas with shining eyes.

"Yes – I read it when I was your age" – said the schoolmaster . . . "but, d'you know, I've forgotten every word . . . it's a sort of Robinson Crusoe story, isn't it?"

"It's ever so much better than Robinson Crusoe! . . ." said Guillou with enthusiasm.

"In what way is it better?"

This direct question sent the boy back into his shell. The vague, almost vacant, look reappeared on his face.

"I always thought it was a sequel to something else" – went on Monsieur Bordas, after a pause.

"It is. You ought to have read *Twenty Thousand Leagues Under the Sea* first, and *Captain Grant's Children*. . . . I haven't read *Twenty Thousand Leagues under the Sea*, but it doesn't really make any difference. You can understand *The Mysterious Island* just the same . . . except where Cyrus Smith makes things like dynamite . . . I always skip those parts."

"Isn't there a shipwrecked man on one of the neighbouring islands whom the engineer's companions discover?"

"Yes, he's called Ayrton, you know. There's a lovely bit when Cyrus Smith says to him – 'If you can cry that means you are a man.' . . ."

Without looking at the boy, Monsieur Bordas took the fat, red-bound book and held it out.

"Try and find the place . . . I seem to remember; there's a picture, I think."

"It's at the end of chapter fifteen," said Guillou.

"Read that page to me . . . it'll take me back to my childhood."

He lit an oil-lamp and settled Guillou at a table covered with Jean-Pierre's ink-stains. The boy began to read in a muffled voice. At first the schoolmaster could catch only one to two words. He was sitting far back in the shadows, scarcely daring to breathe. It was as though he were afraid of startling a wild bird. Gradually, the reader's voice grew stronger and more distinct. . . . He had forgotten now that anyone was listening.

". . . When they reached the spot where the first tall

trees of the forest grew, their leaves faintly stirring in the breeze, the stranger began greedily sniffing the smell which filled the air. He sighed deeply. The planters kept well behind, ready to seize him should he make any attempt to escape. And indeed, the poor wretch was about to plunge into the creek which lay between him and the forest. For a brief moment his legs were like two springs at the moment of release. . . . But almost at once he fell gack, half collapsing, and a large tear welled up in his eye. 'Ah,' exclaimed Cyrus Smith: 'if you can cry, it means that you have once more become a man.' "

"How fine that is!" said Monsieur Bordas. "It all comes back to me now. Isn't the island attacked by convicts?"

"Yes, and it's Ayrton who first catches sight of the black flag. . . . Would you like me to go on reading?"

The schoolmaster pushed his chair still further back. He could, he should, have been lost in wonder at hearing the ardent voice coming from a boy who was generally regarded as an idiot. He could, he should, have rejoiced in the task that had been laid upon him, at the power that was his to save this trembling scrap of humanity. But he heard the boy only through the tumult of his own thoughts. . . . Here he was, a man of forty, burning with desires, bursting with ideas, yet fated never to escape from a schoolhouse in an empty village street. He could understand and appraise all that was printed in the magazine. The smell of its ink and gum was in his nostrils. All the questions of which it treated were familiar to him, though he could talk of them to nobody but Monsieur Lousteau. There was a lot, too, that Léone could have grasped, but she preferred her daily chores. Her mind was growing indolent as her physical activities increased. It had become a matter of pride to her that she could scarcely keep her eyes open when evening came, so tired did she feel. Sometimes she was filled with pity for her husband, for she was too intelligent not to realize that he was suffering. But in Jean-Pierre they would find their compensation. It was her opinion that when a man has reached her husband's age he is willing enough to shift the burden of ambition to the shoulders of his son . . . that was her opinion.

He noticed that the boy, having reached the end of the chapter, had stopped.

"Shall I go on?"

"No," said Monsieur Bordas: "take a rest. You read very well. Would you like me to lend you one of Jean-Pierre's books?"

Guillou jumped up, and once again began to examine

all the volumes, one by one, spelling out their titles in a low voice.

"*Sans famille* . . . is that a nice one?"

"Jean-Pierre used to be very fond of it. But he reads more serious books now."

"D'you think I should understand it?"

"Of course you would! My school work doesn't give me much time for reading nowadays. . . . You shall tell me what it's about, a bit each day. I shall enjoy that."

"That's what you say! . . . but I know you're laughing at me, really. . . ."

Guillou walked over the fireplace. He looked at a photograph leaning against the mirror. It showed schoolboys grouped round two masters wearing pince-nez. Their trousers were stretched tight over their large knees. He asked whether Jean-Pierre was there.

"Yes, in the front row – to the right of the master."

He would have recognized him, thought Guillou, even if he had not been pointed out. Among all the other dim and meaningless faces, this one face glowed. Was it because of all he had been hearing about Jean-Pierre that he thought that? For the first time in his life, he was realizing what a human face could be like. He had often looked long and fondly at pictures, in love with the features of some figure of fiction. But now it suddenly came to him that this boy with the high forehead, the close curls, and the frown between his eyes, was the boy who had actually read these books, worked at this table, slept in this bed.

"Is this room really his very own? Can't anyone come into it if he doesn't want them to?"

He, himself, was never alone except in the lavatory....

The rain was splashing on the roof. How lovely it must be to live shut away among all these books . . . beyond the reach of other people. But Jean-Pierre needed no defences. He was top of his form in every subject. He had even won a prize for gymnastics, Monsieur Bordas had said.

Léone pushed the door open.

"Your mother has come for you, young man."

Once more he followed on behind the schoolmaster carrying the lamp. Once more he crossed the family bedroom. Paula de Cernès was drying her boots at the fire. She must have come by dirty field-paths....

"No need for me to ask whether you got anything out of him. Of course you didn't!"

Monsieur Bordas protested that things hadn't gone badly at all. The boy stood with hanging head while Léone buttoned his cape.

"Would you mind coming outside with me for a moment?" said Paula. "It has left off raining, and I should like to know what you really think."

The schoolmaster took down his mackintosh. His wife followed him into their bedroom. He wasn't going to go stumping the roads at night with that madwoman, was he? He'd be getting himself talked about. . . . All this she asked, but only got a snub for her pains. Paula, who could guess the subject of their whispered conversation, pretended that she had heard nothing. At the front door she once again overwhelmed Léone with protestations of gratitude. Then, with the schoolmaster at her side, she plunged into the damp darkness. She said to Guillou:

"You run along ahead, and don't keep getting under our feet."

Her voice, when she turned to her companion, was firm and determined.

"I want to know the truth, no matter how painful the truth may be to a mother's ears."

He had slowed his pace. Might not Léone be right after all? Whatever happened, they mustn't be seen together crossing the path of light which came from the Hotel Dupuy. But even had he been certain that they would not be seen, he would still have been on the defensive. He had never been anything else with women since the days of his boyhood. It had always been they who sought him out, always he who had run away – and not that he might be the more urgently pursued.

As they approached the Hotel Dupuy, he halted.

"We had better postpone this conversation till to-morrow. Come to my house towards the end of the morning. I finish at the Mairie just before noon."

She knew perfectly well why he did not want to walk further with her. The thought that there was something very like the beginning of a plot between them, filled her with joy.

"Yes," she murmured; "that will be much better."

"Till to-morrow evening, then, Guillaume, my boy. You shall read *Sans famille* to me."

Monsieur Bordas did no more than raise one finger to his beret. Almost at once he was lost to sight, but Paula could still hear, from time to time, the noise made by his stick striking a stone. The boy, too, remained for a few moments motionless in the middle of the road, gazing back at the light which came from Jean-Pierre's home.

His mother took him by the arm. She asked him no questions. There was nothing to be got out of him. Besides, what did she care? To-morrow they were to have their first meeting, their first intimate talk. She gripped Guillou's little hand more tightly than she need have done. The cold of the rain-drenched road struck through her shoes.

"Come to the fire," said Fraülein: "you're soaked to the skin."

Every eye was fixed on him. He would have to answer all their questions.

"Well, so your schoolmaster didn't gobble you up after all?"

He shook his head.

"What did you do for those two hours?"

He did not know what to say. What *had* he done? His mother pinched his arm.

"Didn't you hear? What did you do for those two hours?"

"I shelled beans."

The Baronne raised her hands:

"So he shelled beans for them! A nice thing, I must say!" – she said, unconsciously imitating her Arbis grandchildren. "Do you hear that, Paula? The schoolmaster and his wife sit there gloating, while *my* grandson shells their beans for them! Just what I might have expected. Perhaps they asked you to sweep out the kitchen?"

"No, Mamie . . . I only shelled beans. A lot had gone bad, and I had to sort them out."

"It didn't take them long to size him up!" said Paula.

Fraülein protested:

"I think it was only that they didn't want to scare him the first day."

But the Baronne knew what was to be expected from

people like that once they had got anyone in their clutches.

"No doubt it gives them a great deal of pleasure to play a trick like that on us. But if they think they've got the better of me, they're very much mistaken. I don't mind in the least."

"If they treated Guillou badly . . ." broke in Fraülein sharply . . . "I am very sure that Madame la Baronne would not tolerate it. . . . After all, he is her own grandson. . . ."

Gouillou's voice rose shrill:

"The schoolmaster isn't a bad man!"

"Because he made you shell beans? . . . you like doing servant's work . . . you like being a good-for-nothing. . . . But he's going to make you read, and write and do sums . . . and with him" – went on Paula – "you'll have to watch how you go. Don't forget that he's a schoolmaster!"

In a low, trembling voice Guillou stuck to his point. "He isn't a bad man . . . he's made me read already . . . and he says I read well. . . ."

But his mother, Mamie and Fraûlein had begun bickering again, and were not listening.

All right, then, what did he care? He'd *keep* his secret. The schoolmaster had made him read *The Mysterious Island*. To-morrow he was going to start on *Sans famille*. Every evening, now, he would go to Monsieur Bordas's house. He could look at Jean-Pierre's photograph for as long as he liked. Already he adored Jean-Pierre madly. They would become friends during the summer holidays. He would turn the pages of all Jean-Pierre's books, one by one, the books which Jean-Pierre's hands had touched. It was not because of Monsieur Bordas that his heart was overflowing with happiness, but because of an unknown boy. The sense of delight never left him for the whole evening. It was with him during the interminable meal, at which the irascible gods sat, separated by deserts of silence, during which Guillou could hear Galéas chewing and swallowing. It stayed with him while he groped his way out of his clothes between the dressmaker's dummy and the sewing-machine, while he lay shivering between his stained sheets, when he began his prayers all over again because he had not paid attention to the meaning of the words, and when he had to struggle against the temptation of lying on his stomach. . . . Long after sleep had come, a smile still lit the child's face which was like the face of an old man, with moist and pendulous lip. It was a smile that might have filled his mother with surprise had she been one of those women who tuck their children up in bed, and leave a blessing with them for the night.

About the same time, Léone was breaking in upon her husband's reading.

"Look!" she exclaimed, "what that filthy little creature has done to Jean-Pierre's book! There are finger marks all over it, and even traces of nose-dirt! What can have come over us to lend it to him!"

"There's nothing particularly sacrosanct about them ... you're not the mother of the Messiah!"

Léone, now thoroughly put out, raised her voice:

"I won't have the little horror here again! You can give him his lessons in the schoolroom, in the stables, anywhere you like, but not here!"

Robert shut his book, got up, went across, and sat down beside his wife in front of the fire.

"You're not exactly a model of consistency, are you? Only a little while ago you were blaming me because I showed the old Baronne the door, and now you've got a grievance because I behaved decently to her daughter-in-law. . . . It's the bearded lady that's the trouble . . . it's no use your denying it . . . poor bearded lady!"

"And don't *you* deny that it's a fine feather in your cap!" – said Léone, giving him a kiss. "I know you. What a scalp to hang at your belt – the lady from the great house!"

"I really don't think I could bring it off, not even if I wanted to."

"Oh, I know all about what differentiates men" – said Léone: "you've explained it to me often enough.

There are those who are always ready for it, and those who aren't...."

"Yes, and those who are always ready, don't, really, live for anything else, because, whatever people may say, it's about the pleasantest thing in life."

"And those who aren't" – said Léone, continuing with the litany (there were several "gags", dating from the days when they were first engaged, which they were always trotting out, because they could always be relied upon to bring every argument to a happy end) ... "devote themselves to God, to Science, or to Literature...."

"Or to their own sex," wound up Robert.

She laughed, and went into the bathroom, leaving the door open. As he was undressing, he called out to her:

"You know, I wouldn't have minded taking on the little wretch ... might have been interesting."

She came back, looking, with her rather lifeless hair braided in a plait, pleased with herself and rather appealing in her faded red flannel nightgown.

"Then you've given up the idea?"

"If I have, it's not because of the bearded lady! But I've been thinking. . . . I'll have to go back on my promise. I ought never to have given it in the first place. We mustn't have anything to do with the great house. The class-war isn't just something in a textbook. It's part of our daily life, and it ought to control our every action."

He broke off. She was squatting on her heels, cutting her toenails. She was quite clearly not listening.

... One can't talk to women.... The mattress creaked under the weight of his large body. She snuggled up against him and blew out the candle. The room was filled with the smell of burned wick. It was a smell they both of them loved, because it was the precursor of love-making and sleep.

"No, not to-night" – said Léone.

They whispered for a while.

"Stop talking now, I'm going to sleep."

"Just one more thing: how on earth am I going to get that urchin off my hands?"

"All you've got to do is to write a note to the bearded lady, explaining all about the class-war. She'll understand all right. . . . After all, she *was* a Mademoiselle Meulière! . . . We'll send one of the kids round with it to-morrow. . . . Look, it's hardly dark at all!"

Cocks were crowing to one another. In the linen-closet of the great house, where Fraülein had forgotten to draw the curtains, the moon shone down on Guillou, a pale little ghost perched on his chamber-pot. Behind him, armless, headless, stood the dummy which no one ever used.

CHAPTER IV

IV

THE note delivered by one of the schoolchildren had brought his mother and Mamie much earlier that usual from their rooms. They had the terrible appearance of old people early in the morning, before they have washed, and while their discoloured teeth, embedded in pink, are still reposing in tumblers of water by their beds. Mamie's scalp looked smooth and polished between her thin strands of faded hair, and her empty mouth made it seem as though she were sucking in her cheeks. They were both talking at the same time. Galéas, seated at table, between his two hounds – whose jaws snapped whenever he threw them a scrap of food – was drinking his coffee as though it hurt him. To see him, one would think that every mouthful was an agony. It was Guillaume's firm conviction that the enormous Adam's apple prevented the food from going down. He kept his mind concentrated on his father. He did not want to understand the meaning of the heated words now passing between his mother and Mamie on the subject of the note. But he knew already that he would never again enter Jean-Pierre's room.

"That wretched little Communist teacher's nothing to

do with me!" exclaimed Mamie. "It's *you* he's written to. This snub is aimed at you, my dear."

"What do you mean – snub? He is reading me a lesson. It is a lesson I needed, and I'm glad of it. I believe in the class-war just as much as he does. I didn't mean him any harm. Still, I did urge him to betray his own people."

"What on earth you're getting at, my poor dear, I do *not* know!"

"Here's a young man with all his life before him, and every reason to hope for a brilliant future. And what do I do? I try to compromise him in the eyes of his comrades and his Party leaders. . . . And for what, I ask you? . . . For the sake of a little backward degenerate. . . ."

"I am present, Paula."

She guessed at, rather than heard, her husband's protest. He was still sitting crouched over his bowl of bread and milk. When he grew excited, his thick tongue gave passage only to a confused muddle of sound. Raising his voice, he added:

"Guillaume happens to be present, too."

"The things one's got to listen to!" – exclaimed Fraûlein, and vanished into the scullery.

By this time, the old Baronne had recovered her breath.

"So far as I know, Guillaume is your son too!"

Hatred had quickened the senile jerking of the aged head which was bare and bald and prepared already for the nothingness of death.

Paula whispered in her ear:

"Just look at them both – the original and the copy. It's extraordinary how alike they are!"

The Baronne straightened her back, looked her daughter-in-law up and down without replying, and then, with not a word to Guillou, got up and left the kitchen. The child's grey little face expressed nothing at all. There was a fog outside, and, since Fraülein never washed the one and only window, almost all the light in the room came from the flickering logs in the grate. . . . The two hounds with their muzzles on their paws, and the rough-hewn legs of the enormous table, looked for a moment almost as though they were on fire.

Not another word was spoken. Paula had gone too far, as she fully realized; had affronted the great army of her husband's race, his thousand sleeping ancestors. Galéas uncurled his long legs, scrambled to his feet, wiped his mouth with the back of his hand, and asked the boy whether he had got his cape. He fastened it round the scrawny, birdlike neck, and took Guillou's hand in his. He kicked the two dogs awake. They leaped, fawning on him, all eagerness to follow. Fraülein asked where they were off to. Paula took the words out of his mouth:

"Oh, to the churchyard, of course!"

Yes, that was where they were going. A red sun was struggling with the fog which might lift later, or dissolve in rain. Guillou clung to his father's hand, but very soon had to let it go because it was so damp. Not a word did they exchange until they reached the church. The family tomb of the Cernès stood against the churchyard wall from which the eye could look across the Ciron valley. Galéas went off to fetch a spade from the sacristy. The boy sat down on a gravestone at some little distance from the tomb. He pulled the hood of his cape over his head, then moved no more. . . . Monsieur Bordas didn't want to have anything to do with him. The fog was acting like a sounding-board. He could hear a distant waggon, a crowing cock, the monotonous drone of a motor-car, above the unbroken threshing of the mill-wheel, and the roar of the weir, near which, in Summer time, the village boys bathed naked. A robin sang quite close to him. The migrant birds he loved had flown. Monsieur Bordas didn't want to have anything to do with him. Not a soul, anywhere, wanted him. "I don't care", he said in a low voice, and then, again, as though in challenge to some unseen enemy – "I don't care!" What a noise the weir was making – it was less than a kilometre away as the crow flies. A sparrow winged its way out of the church through the broken window.

"The Good God isn't there" – that was what Mamie said: "They have taken the Good God away. . . ." He was nowhere else, only up in the sky. Dead children are like angels, with pure and shining faces. Guillou's tears, said Mamie, were dirty tears. The more he cried, the filthier his face became, because his grubby hands smeared it with earth. When he got home, his mother would say . . . Mamie would say . . . Fraülein would say. . . .

Monsieur Bordas wasn't going to have anything to do with him. He would never again go into Jean-Pierre's room. Jean-Pierre. Jean-Pierre Bordas. How strange to love a boy whom one has never seen, and never will see. 'If he had met me, he would have thought me ugly, dirty, stupid.' That was what his mother told him everyday: "you're ugly, dirty, stupid." Jean-Pierre Bordas would never know that Guillaume de Cernès was ugly, dirty, stupid – a ragamuffin. And he was something else, too. What was the word his mother had used just now? – a word which had struck his father like a stone? He tried to remember, and could think only of "regenerate". It was some word like "regenerate".

To-night he would fall asleep, but not at once. He would have to wait for sleep, wait through a whole night like last night when he had been trembling with happiness. He had fallen asleep thinking that when he woke he would see Monsieur Bordas again, that, when evening came, he would sit in Jean-Pierre's room and start to read *Sans famille*. . . . If only he could believe that to-night everything would be as it had been then! . . . He got to his feet, made his way round the Cernès tomb, clambered over the wall, and took the path which went steeply downhill towards the Ciron.

Galéas turned his head and saw that the boy was no longer there. He went to the wall and looked over it. The little hood was moving among the vine-rows, getting further and further away. He threw his spade aside, and started off down the same path. When he was no more than a few yards from the boy, he slowed his pace. Guillou had thrown back his hood. He was not wearing a beret. Between his large, projecting ears his cropped head looked very small. His legs were like two twigs ending in enormous boots. His chicken-neck stuck out above the cape. With his eyes Galéas devoured the little shambling creature, the tiny shrewmouse with marks of blood upon it made by the trap from which it had escaped. It was his own son, his image in the flesh, with a whole life to live, yet now, already, burdened with a long-borne weight of suffering. But the torment had only just begun. The torturers would gain new strength. Those of childhood are different from those of youth: and there would be still others when he had become a man full grown. Could he learn to be numb and sottish? Would he have to defend himself, at every moment of his life, against the woman who would be always there, the woman with the Gorgon's face blotched with bilious yellow? Hatred caught at his breath, but, more than hatred, shame, because it was he who had been that woman's torturer. Only once had he taken her in his arms, only once. She was, now, like a bitch confined – not for a few days only. Through all her youth it had gone on, and for years and years she would go howling for the absent male. . . . With what fantasies . . . what actions . . . had he, Galéas, cheated hunger. . . . Every night, yes, every night, and in the morning, too. . . . Such would be the lot of this abortion born of their one embrace, and now running, now hurrying – to what? Did he know? Though the child had not once turned his head, perhaps he was conscious of his father's presence. Galéas was persuaded that it was so. 'He knows I am behind him. He takes no pains to hide himself from me, no, nor to cover his tracks. He is as a guide, leading me to where he wants me to be with him.' Galéas could not bring himself to face the issue to which these last two of the Cernès line were hastening. A tremble of alder leaves spoke of the nearby river. Not now was it the King of the Alders who, in a final gallop, was pursuing the boy, but the boy now who was leading his uncrowned and insulted father towards the sleeping waters of the weir, the pool in which the village boys, in summer, bathed naked. They were close now to the watery confines of that kingdom where never more would they be harassed by wife or mother. They would be delivered from the Gorgon: they would sleep.

They had reached the shade of the tall pines on the river bank. The still living bracken fronds were almost as high as Guillou, whose cropped head Galéas could scarcely see emerging from their tangled wilderness. At a turning of the sandy path the boy once more vanished from sight. They might have met some resin-gatherer, the muleteer from the mill, a sportsman out after woodcock. But every witness had withdrawn from this small corner of the world that the act might be accomplished which these two were fated to perform – one leading the other – or urging him forward unwillingly – who would ever know? There was none to see them, but only the giant pines crowding about the weir. They burned during the following August, left too long untapped. For a long while they spread their calcined limbs above the sleeping water: for a long while they reared against the sky their blackened faces.

The accepted view was that Galéas had jumped into the water to save his son, that the boy had clung about his neck and pulled him down. Such vague rumours as had at first been current were soon silenced by the touching story of a father done to death by his small son's clutching hands. Some might shake their heads and say . . . "Well, I don't feel sure that it happened like that" . . . but the true explanation no one could well imagine. How should anyone suspect a father who loved his boy, and took him every day when he went to the churchyard? . . . "Monsieur Galéas may have been a bit simple, but he had his wits about him, all the same, and there never was a sweeter-natured man."

No one grudged Fraülein the cape which she had taken, sodden with water, from Guillou's body. . . . The old Baronne was happy to think that Cernès would descend to the Arbis children, and that she would be quit, once and for all, of Paula to whom the Meulières had offered a home. She was, as they put it, back on their hands. But she had a malignant tumour. On the glossy walls, in the stifling atmosphere of the hospital (the nurse forever coming in with the basin whether she wanted it or not, and even if she was too tired to open her eyes – and the morphine which was so bad for her liver – and the visits of her aunt always worrying over the terrible expense, which was quite useless anyhow, because the end was a foregone conclusion) – on the glossy walls she sometimes saw, as on a screen, Galéas's shaggy head, and the brat looking up from a torn book, an ink-stained exercise, with his dirty, anxious face. Perhaps she imagined these things? She saw, in fancy, the boy creeping close to the bank, shivering because he was afraid, not of death, but of the cold – and his father tiptoeing behind him.... At that point she hesitated. Had he pushed him, or plunged after him? – or had he taken the small boy in his arms, saying, "Hold tight to me, and don't look." ... Paula did not know, nor ever would. She was happy to think that her own death was close at hand. She kept on telling the nurse that the morphine made her feel ill, that her liver could not stand any more injections. She wanted to drain her cup to the dregs – not that she believed in an unseen world whither our victims precede us, where we can fall at the knees of those who were confided to our care, and have, through our fault, been lost. ... It never occurred to her that she might be judged. She stood at no bar save that of her own conscience. She was absolved in her own sight from the horror she had felt for a son who was the image of a hated father. She had spewed up the Cernès family, because neausea is something that one cannot control. But it was of her own free-will that she had consented to share the bed of a half-impotent monster. She had allowed him to take her in his arms, and that, in her eyes, was the crime for which there was no pardon.

Sometimes the pain was so acute that she could not resist the morphine's promise of a moment's respite. In those lucid intervals she thought of all the lives she might have had. In fancy she was Robert Bordas's wife, surrounded by a brood of healthy boys, whose lower lips did not hang down, who did not slaver. Each night he took her in his arms, and she slept pressed close to his body. She dreamed of men's hairy pelts, and of their smell. She never knew what time of day or night it was. Pain knocked at the door: pain entered in and took its lodgement, and started slowly to eat her life away.

That a mother should be ashamed of her son, or of her grandson, should not, thought Fraülein, be permitted. She could not forgive her mistress for having shed so few tears over Galéas and Guillou gone, for having, perhaps, been happy at their going. The Arbis family would never let her die in peace at Cernès. 'Suppose I told Madame la Baronne what I heard their chauffeur say after the funeral – about how could anyone think that a woman of her age could possibly need a gardener, an assistant gardener, and two indoor servants, and all the expenses of a house? That is how their minds are working. I know that they have been enquiring about terms for aged pensioners, of the Ladies of the Presentation at Verdelais.' . . . The Baronne kept turning and twisting her bald vulture's head among the pillows. She would refuse to go to the Ladies of the Presentation. . . . "If the Arbis have decided, Madame la Baronne will go, and I with her.

Madame la Baronne has never been able to say 'no' to the Arbis. They frighten her: and, I confess, they frighten me...."

Thursday: a respite from the children. But the schoolmaster had his work to do at the Mairie. Hurriedly he passed a washing-glove over his face which was puffy with sleep. What point was there in shaving? Nobody who mattered would see him. He did not put on walking-shoes. In weather like this a pair of socks would keep his feet warm, and, with clogs on, he need not fear getting them wet. Léone had gone to the butcher's. He could hear the rain upon the roof. There was a puddle right across the road. When Léone got back, she would say – "What are you thinking about?" – and he would answer "nothing". They had not so much as mentioned Guillou's name since the day when the two bodies had been fished out of the mill-pond. Then, for the first and only time, he had said: "The lad killed himself, or else his father..." and Léone with a shrug had muttered – "Do you really think so?" From then on, they had never mentioned the boy's name. But Léone knew that the little skeleton in cape and hood was for ever wandering through the school, and creeping about the playground, not joining in the games. Robert Bordas went into Jean-Pierre's room, and took up *The Mysterious Island*. The book opened of itself. "The poor wretch was just about to plunge into the creek which lay between him and the forest. For a moment, his legs were like two springs at the moment of release. . . . But almost at once he fell back, half collapsing, and a large tear welled up in his eye. 'Ah!', cried Cyrus Smith, 'if you can cry, that means that you have once more become a man!' ". . . Monsieur Bordas sat down on Jean-Pierre's bed. The thick red book with its golden titling lay open on his knee. . . . Guillou. . . . In that suffering body a human spirit had laid unawakened. . . . How wonderful to have helped it into consciousness. That, maybe, was the task which Robert Bordas had been born into this world to accomplish. At the Ecole Normale, one of the professors had taught Etymology – *Instituteur* – schoolmaster – from *Institutor* – one who builds, one who instructs, one who sets the human spirit in a man. A fine word. He might meet other Guillous on his road. For the sake of the child whom he had left to die, he would never again refuse to give of his utmost to those who came to him. But none of them would be that same small boy who now was dead because Monsieur Bordas had one day taken him in, and, the next, had thrown him out like a stray puppy which he had warmed a moment at his fire. He had sent him into the darkness for ever. But was it really darkness? He strained his eyes in an effort to see beyond material things, beyond the walls and the furniture of this, his house, beyond the tiled roof, beyond the star-pointed night, beyond the Winter constellations. He sat there, seeking the kingdom of the spirit where, rapt away into eternity, the boy could see him still, and, on his cheek, stubbly with unshaven beard, a tear he had not thought to wipe away.

The Spring grass strayed into the churchyard at Cernès. . . . Roots took hold upon the untended graves; moss made the epitaphs unreadable. Since the day when Galéas had taken his small son by the hand, choosing that they should sleep together, there had been nobody at Cernès to concern himself about the dead.